Sincerely,

The Invisible Girl

Thank you for the love and support. It's greatly appreciated.

Sincerely,
Antonia Harry

Sincerely,
The Invisible Girl

By: Antonia Harris

Copyright © 2018 by Antonia Harris

In CTRL Publishing & Company LLC

P.O. Box 87306

Baton Rouge, La 70879

Sincerely, The Invisible Girl

By: Antonia Harris

Printed in the United States of America

ISBN- 978-0-692-13877-9

    All rights reserved solely by the author. The author guarantees all contents are original and do not infringe upon the legal rights of any other person or work. No part of this book may be reproduced or transmitted in any form or by any means, electronic or mechanical, including photocopying or recording, without permission in writing from the publisher.

"Leave a place better than you found it."
-Debra Thomas
This one's for you Mom!

"Call 911! Call 911!" bawled mom. I was scared and terrified. The only thing I could do was run back into the bedroom to ask, "What's the number again?" As the question rolled off my tongue, the room began to spin. All I could see was my mother's body dangling on the bed while this monster was on top of her trying to choke the life out of her. How could he do that to her? How could I forget the number? I didn't know what to do. I just froze. I can't believe I just stood there and looked at my mom's lifeless body. She couldn't fight anymore. However, I still tried to protect my brothers. Oh no! My brothers! They have to witness this, again. Why does she keep allowing him to do this to her? How could I have protected them while I was afraid myself? I would try to shield their faces, preventing them from watching our mother get hit by their father. Yes, it was their father. I hated him! Finally, I remembered the number. It took little time for the police to come and arrest that grimy, hateful monster. As the two officers entered the house, one was a huge Caucasian man, and the other one was a short-statured, bald African American man. They immediately asked, "What's going on here?" That coward had the nerve to tell the officers everything was fine. I was furious on the inside. I saw red, and I blurted out, "Liar!" Immediately, my mother covered my mouth and specified, "Josh, Troy, everything is okay over here. We got into a pretty bad argument, and Jen got scared. Sorry to bother you guys." Josh and Troy looked puzzled as Troy asked, "Are you sure, Marcie, because your neck looks a little red." Josh added, "Don't be afraid. We can take this bastard away for the night." Josh and Troy had been notified several times before about the altercations between my mother and Gary's nasty, grimy self. As the officers were speaking to my mother, Gary stood there with a smirk on his face, looking like the Devil. My brothers, Lil Gary and Torian, stood in the corner of the living room with looks of confusion and fear of their father and the police. Mom would threaten to call the police on them when they would misbehave. In return, they had developed a great fear of the police. My little brothers were so bad that I was glad Mom used something to terrify them. Just like they loved to torture me. Mom finally agreed with the officers to allow Gary to leave for the night. She realized they should probably talk in the morning, once everything calmed down between them. As the officers escorted Gary out of the house, Gary glared at me so coldly that it sent shivers down my back. That man was evil, and I needed him to know it. The moment he walked passed me, I yelled, "Devil!" Troy turned around and gave me a grin, as Mom scorned me for being disrespectful to adults. "Stay in a child's place," Mom said. "He shouldn't put his hands on you then," I said with an attitude. My mother was a gorgeous woman, with golden brown skin, a short pixie cut, and a beautiful hourglass figure. Every man in the neighborhood would flirt with her, and she would smile and keep moving. I never understood why she chose Gary because she was so much better than him. Mom then did something she had never done to me before, "Pop!" She slapped me. Then she walked out before I could even say anything back. I was known for talking back to adults even though it would result in a slap or a pop. I felt like I needed to defend myself. I stormed out of the room while pushing my brothers out of the way and stomping my feet as I slammed my bedroom door. She yelled, "Don't slam my door! You can't afford to buy another one!" As she was talking, I whispered a naughty word as I began to throw things around my room. That was my thing. I would throw things. I couldn't express to her how I felt without getting hit or punished. That night, I cried to myself while trying to fall asleep. All I could think about was, Why didn't my mother love me the way she loves my brothers? She would've never slapped them for taking up for her. She would probably love the fact that her sons are protecting her. At that moment, I decided to take out my diary and write. It usually helped me feel better. First, I had to rummage through the items on the floor and try to find it. I threw it somewhere when I went on my rampage of destruction. There it goes: a pink floral diary with a gold plate and a missing lock. I had a hard time keeping up with my things. However, I could never lose my diary. It was where I kept my most significant, most profound, and darkest secrets away from everybody. It was my safe place. I could use curse words and not get in trouble for it. I could say mean things about people and not hurt their feelings. I could also say the things about my family that I couldn't tell anyone else.

Dear Diary,

Is my Mom mad at me because I couldn't remember the phone number to 911? I was so afraid that he was going to kill her. I am too young to raise my evil brothers; they don't even listen to me when I'm watching them for Mom. Do you know what they did to me one day? Mom was at the store, and I was watching them. They decided to place toothpicks everywhere they knew I would walk. They started in the dining room area, went to my room, and then went all the way to their room. You know what? I stepped on every last toothpick. They laughed and teased me for weeks after that! I can't stand them! Lil bad tails. Shoot! I get mad every time I think about their trifling selves. I love them, but I don't think I can take care of them. Oh, and Gary, ole nasty, grimy self, had the nerve to give me an evil glare as Mr. Josh and Mr. Tory walked him out of the house. He doesn't belong here anyway. He doesn't do anything but hurt my momma. He's stupid, and I hope he dies. Well, I don't want my brothers to be sad, but they'll be better off anyway, and Mom will be happy again. I can't remember the last time she was pleasant. While she's over here slapping me, she needs to leave his hateful self, so she doesn't get hurt. I am so angry with her, but I'll get over it. I always do. It's not the first time, and it won't be the last time. Thanks for listening.

Sincerely,

The Invisible Girl

Chapter 1

It's officially summer! Two months have passed since Gary's ole raggedy self tried to kill my momma. It seemed like things were back to normal. Summer days were so different for the Claiborne/Washington household. It was consumed with baseball and softball schedules along with all the neighborhood boys coming over to play basketball in our backyard on the black dirt. The black dirt wasn't anything nice. Once it got on your clothes, they were permanently stained. Everybody knew that when they came over, they needed to wear their "play clothes" and old dirty tennis shoes. Summers in rural Louisiana was very hot and humid with hot days and even hotter nights. If you ever come to Louisiana, please be prepared to be WET, slimy, and icky from sweat because of the humidity. During the summers, we got to go to Ms. Mark's house around the block to get "frozen cups." Frozen cups are these frozen, delectable drinks made from Kool-Aid, sugar (lots of it), and this syrupy topping in a white Styrofoam cup. We would buy them daily for $0.25. Frozen cups from Ms. Mark were the best $0.25 I ever spent. Lil' Gary would pay for one and leave with three or four. That boy was so slick; he would steal your glasses off your face and be gone before you realized he had taken them. Then, on special occasions, we would go to the local grocery store, Ralphies, and get snowcones from the stand right outside Ralphies. It had so many flavors on the menu that it was hard to choose which one to get. There were flavors such as bubblegum, strawberry cheesecake, ice cream, and wedding cake. The wedding cake was my favorite, and I would get the cream on top. Oh, and I can't forget to mention Icees. Oh yes! Icees were great for those sweltering days on the softball field. As you can see, the Louisiana heat ain't no joke. You have multiple delicious, cold, frosty options to deal with it.

On the first day of summer, I was so excited to be officially done with the 7th grade and Mrs. Smith's stinky-breath self. When I say you can smell Mrs. Smith's breath down the 7th-grade hallway, you better believe it. Let me not forget to mention she had the nerve to teach English. Yes, English! This subject required her to talk the ENTIRE class period. It was the worst class ever for me. I am so excited that I can finally use my sense of smell again. Don't get me started on that lady. I'm trying to enjoy my summer and not think about that dragon-breath woman. I woke up around 9 a.m., with the sun blinding me. The ceiling fan was pumping, and the floor fan was on a high. Unbelievably, I was still hot. We didn't have a central air conditioning unit, and mom didn't put a window air conditioning unit in my room. As I stated earlier, the heat was disrespectful. I wasn't that mad about it because the way the sun hit my pink wall was right. Last summer, mom and I painted my room pink. My cousin India gave me all of her old white bedroom furniture, and it fit my room perfectly. India was also getting other new, fancy things. I would always be excited to receive all of her hand-me-downs. She kept all of her belongings in great condition. In fact, they still looked brand new when I got them. It was like they were brand new. In return, I also made sure I kept them up too. So this meant NO boys were allowed in my room, especially Lil Gary and Torian's ole bad self. My room was my haven, and I didn't need any stinky boys dirtying up my favorite place. As I got out of my bed to go to the bathroom, I saw some red spots on my yellow sheets. I immediately panicked. I ran to the bathroom to see what was going on. All kinds of thoughts began going through my head. "Did I pee in the bed? If I did, why was it red? Wait, are my insides bleeding?" I yelled, "Momma! Momma!" Then I heard, "Girl, shut up, with all that hollering in my house!" "Uhh, you ain't my daddy," I whispered. I wish I could be brave enough to tell people like Gary how I feel to their face. He makes me so angry; why does my momma allow him to say anything to me. He's not my daddy. As I was about to yell for my mom again, Torian came to the door to tell me she wasn't at home.

Torian was my baby brother. He was the sweetest person to me when Lil Gary wasn't around. Torian was five years old. He was very athletic for his age. He was quiet, yet he didn't let anybody mess with him. He was a little firecracker. "Thanks, Tor." At that moment, I didn't know what to do. "Is this what Keshawn and Traci were talking about at school, that made their boobs grow big? Will my boobs grow to be big now? If they do, that is awesome. That means the boys will like me and I won't be invisible anymore." I started to get excited! "I will no longer be invisible, and I'll finally have boobs! I think I started my period." My Aunt Keisha once sat me down to explain the female body and what happens when you have a menstrual cycle. She explained to me that another name for it is a period. I decided not to panic and looked for something to stop the bleeding. My mom had two separate boxes that she used when she started her period. I went to see what I could use. As I was looking through the first box, I heard. "Hurry up in the doggone bathroom, girl. You don't pay bills around here." I whispered, "You don't, either." There went Gary's stupid self again. I thought to myself, "Why can't he ever call me by my name?" He would always refer to me as "girl." Maybe he didn't know my name. That was good! I didn't want him to know anything about me, especially what was happening. The first box was pink. The cover read, "Tampons." When I opened the box, I pulled out a long, skinny tool wrapped in white paper. It felt hard. When I opened it, there was something that appeared to be a thick Q-tip surrounded by a white cardboard box. "What the heck am I supposed to do with this?" I immediately started looking for directions, to see how I could use this piece of cardboard. "Do I have to put this hard thing inside of me?" I froze. I decided to take a look at the longer box that read, "Panty Liners." I said to myself, "Oh, that's simple." I threw my old underwear in the trashcan and used my first panty liner for my first period. Instantly, I felt like a woman. "Today is going to be a good day," I thought to myself. Then, I remembered the stains on the bed. "Oh no! The stains on my bed!" I didn't want my mom to think that I had peed the bed and punish me. I also didn't want those brothers of mine to find out about this, which would give them another reason to tease me. I used some dishwashing liquid and hot water to clean the stain. "Whew, glad that's up before mom gets home!" I got ready for the day and fixed me some Cookie Crisp. This was my favorite breakfast cereal. Oh the taste of chocolate chip cookies soaked up in milk sounds so good me. Mom only bought them occasionally, so I had to take advantage of savoring them before Lil Gary, ole greedy behind, ate them all. That boy knew he could eat up all of the good food mom bought for the house. He decided he wanted to run the streets all day and then come home to eat us out of house and home. He was four years younger than me, but you would've thought he was grown the way he ran the streets. I had to sit at the dining room table watching ESPN highlights all morning because the mean ole monster, Gary, was watching TV in the living room. The living room and dining area were all together in one room. I also didn't have a choice of what I could watch when Big Gary was in here watching TV. He was always at home. It was as if he didn't have a job. I don't know what he did for living besides get on my dang nerves. I don't believe he had a real job. He reminded me of Tommy from the funny show Martin. He would leave for weeks and come back for months. My poor momma had to do everything while this lazy man did nothing. Gary was a tall, brown-skinned man with a bald, shiny head. He dressed like he was trapped in the '70s. "Don't forget to wash that bowl girl!" That's what he yelled as I was getting up from the dining room table. I wish I could eat in my room, but my momma don't play that. Kids had to eat at the table for every meal, even snacks. I couldn't wait to be an adult so I could eat anywhere I wanted to. I would even eat in the bathroom, just because I could. As I was getting ready to go outside, I heard, "Jen! Brang yo tail in here right now!" All I could think was,

"Oh no, what did I do now?" I slowly crept into my mom's room, which was next door to mine. I walked so slow it took me like five minutes to get there. "Jen, why were you in my stuff? Why is my tampon and panty liner wrapper in the trash can?" At that moment, I was speechless. It was easy for me to tell her the truth, but I was too petrified to let her know what was going on. "Jen, if you don't open your mouth, I'll open it for you." I knew she would because Momma didn't play that mess. "I started my period," I uttered. "What? How do you know it's a period?" "Keisha explained it to me," I replied. "Girl, you didn't have a period yet. Stay out of my stuff! Oh, and since you want to tell stories, go write one in your room because you can't go outside," Mom said. "But Mom-" Before I could finish my sentence, she yelled, "Don't 'but' me; do as I say! The more I teach you, the dumber I get!" I left, disappointed and confused. Maybe it hadn't been my period. Maybe I had rubbed myself with toilet paper too hard in the middle of the night. I was known for making up stories, so it was hard for my family to believe me. Sometimes, I would make up elaborate stories and share them with everyone. Eventually, I would start believing my own made-up stories. However, this time, I knew I couldn't be making up a story with actual red spots on my sheets and in my underwear. Maybe telling stories too often kept my mom from ever again believing what I said. I still didn't know what the red spots were. Nevertheless, I decided to take mom's advice and just write in my diary.

Dear Diary,

I thought this was it. I thought I was becoming a woman. I knew that I started my period. All the boys like Keshawn and Traci because they have boobs and are gorgeous. They have their periods. Keshawn was even having sex with boys. At least, that's what I heard. I'm invisible to boys. I'm long, skinny, four-eyed, big nosed, and flat chested. The boys make fun of me because I have big hands and feet, and at times, I'm clumsy, like that time we were in the breezeway during lunchtime, and we were close to the vending machines. I was going to meet up with Traci and Keshawn after lunch. As I was passing David and his crew, I tripped over my shoelaces and fell in front of the entire 7th-grade student body. It was as if I fell in slow motion. I could remember David covering his mouth while he was laughing during my fall. David was one beautiful chocolate teenager. I wish he were my boyfriend. But he's not going to like me if I still look like a string bean. I think I got my hopes up about becoming a woman for nothing. My mom told me it wasn't time for my period. Well, better luck next time. I guess.

Sincerely,

    The Invisible Girl

On the following day, I woke up to more red spots on my sheets. Maybe this is a bad dream. However, all I knew was that I couldn't tell mom. I didn't want her to fuss at me again. I decided to sneak a few of her panty liners and hide the spotted underwear as I cleaned the spots up. I couldn't get myself in trouble over another accident. Three days later, I didn't see any more spots of blood.

Chapter 2

Around June 20th, I was definitely about to become visible to other people. I was finally getting contacts. No more "four eyes" for me. I was going to look like a real teenager, rather than Myrtle Urkel, Steve Urkel's cousin, from Family Matters. I was tired of looking like a little girl. I wanted David and his friends to notice how mature I looked. I wanted a boyfriend my 8th-grade year. I was tired of getting looked over because of my flat boobs and glasses. My peers also teased me for being awkward. That was okay because I accepted the fact that I was different. I didn't want to be awkward and ugly, though. For that reason, my glasses had to go. My optometrist, Dr. Wilson, was a very nice man. He made my visits very entertaining. He taught me to accept people for their differences. Dr. Wilson was different. He had Tourette's syndrome. Tourette's syndrome is a nerve disorder where the individual with the disorder experiences involuntary movements and speech. Dr. Wilson experienced involuntary movements in the middle of our appointments. The muscles in his face and shoulders would jerk. When I was younger, it frightened me. However, I was older and more mature now. After my first appointment, he explained the syndrome to me. I've been comfortable with it ever since. During the appointment, I expressed my excitement about finally being able to wear contacts to Dr. Wilson. He educated me on the importance of keeping my contacts clean to protect my eyes. Before leaving, I hugged Dr. Wilson and ran towards the receptionist to pick up my contacts. My first day wearing contacts was awesome. When it was time to take them out, the struggle was real. I tried, and I tried, but the contacts were glued to my eyes. I couldn't tell Mom I was having trouble taking my contacts out because she was going to make me wear my glasses again. I struggled for two hours as I roamed back and forth in my room, talking to myself. I stared at my white vanity and started crying. I felt hopeless because I couldn't take them out of my dang eyes. It got worse and worse; I started scratching my eyeballs, trying to remove them. As soon as the tears started streaming down my eyes, the contacts loosened up. They eventually became easier to remove. I was staring at myself in the in the mirror with pale skin and red, puffy eyes. Nevertheless, there was a smirk on my face. The smirk was because I accomplished the first task of removing these contacts by myself. That night, I slept like a baby. However, the next day brought on a new struggle. I couldn't put them dang things in my eyes! "Oh No! Not again! Please tell me this isn't so. I can't get them in my eyes." As I was stretching, pulling, and cleaning the contacts, "Rip!" I tore one of the lenses. "Calm down Jen; you can do this." Pop! "Wait not another one. Okay, relax. Mom bought you a box with 12 lenses. You can try again." "Jen, come on, I'm ready to go to Shell's house." My Aunt Shell was one of my favorite aunts who wasn't really my aunt. She and my mom were first cousins, but they acted like they were sisters. My cousin India was Aunt Shell's daughter. India just had a baby girl named Gracie. Mom was very excited to meet Gracie for the first time, and so was I.

Mom was leaving the bad-tail boys at home, and she and I were going to meet Gracie. I loved going to Aunt Shell's house. It was a large white house with very fancy furniture and fancy trinkets. She even had an all-white room that no one could enter unless it was a special holiday. "Jen, bring your tail on so we can go," hollered Mom. As I was about to reply, she stormed into my room to rush me. "Put them thangs in your eyes and come on!" She looked around, "Why the hell you got all these empty containers of contacts on the floor?" "I can't put them in," I cried. She replied, "Girl, come on! India can help you put them in." I was so nervous my hands started shaking. During the entire three-minute ride, Mom fussed about the money she spent on the contacts and how I was going to wear my glasses because I was wasting her doggone money. She jumped out the car, fussing all the way to the door as I dragged my feet. "This girl is wasting my damn money; she done went through six pairs of contacts. India, please help this damn girl before I kill her." I walked in the house with my head down, feeling defeated once again. "Come on, it's okay, I'll help you," said India. India was so nice and understanding as she was teaching me how to put in the contacts. I was so excited, receiving them, I guess I didn't pay enough attention to Dr. Wilson on how to use them. India had just had a baby, but she was patient with me. I eventually stopped shaking. That was still odd because India had never, ever really been nice to me. Maybe Gracie had softened her up. She hardly ever acknowledged me, maybe because I was the little, lame cousin. India was three years older than me and very popular. She wore the best name-brand clothes, she had the popular friends, and everyone loved her. I was jealous, yet I wanted to be India at the same time. She would give me all her old clothes. However, I still wasn't cool like her when I wore them. I was still invisible. "Thanks, India! I think I got it for real this time." She replied, "I hope so because you know how crazy your mom is." We always joked about my crazy momma. Now, it was finally time for me to meet baby Gracie. Gracie was the most beautiful baby I'd ever seen. She was a tiny, golden baby with beautiful gray eyes. She was wearing an adorable white dress. She looked angelic. I was afraid to hold her because she was so tiny. I stared at her while she lay on Aunt Shell's large, king-sized bed, sleeping peacefully. As I was staring, I could still hear my mom complaining about me and the contacts. She wouldn't leave it alone. I understand that the contacts cost a lot of money! Couldn't she give me another chance and stop talking about it? It wasn't like she had really paid a lot of money for them; I had Medicaid, shoot. We stayed over for a few more hours, and then she drove home in silence. All I could think to myself was, "I have to prove her wrong."

Dear Diary,

I think I hate my mom. She is always fussing and embarrassing me. Okay, I know I ruined six contact lenses, but damn! Yep, I said damn! It isn't like she's going to do anything about it anyway. She's always telling people what I can and can't do. I'm so glad that India was there to have my back. The way she taught me how to put my contacts in was easy. I'm going to show Mom; I can do it now! Oh yeah, I met my baby cousin Gracie today! She is beautiful. I can't believe India had a baby. Maybe I should have a baby? Naw, I don't want a baby. Lol. India is good at everything she does. Being a great mom will undoubtedly fall under her belt. I want to be good at something so that everybody will like me.

Sincerely,

The Invisible Girl

That night, I struggled to remove my contact lenses again. I was too emotionally drained to cry or even throw a tantrum for myself. I was exhausted; I fell asleep on the vanity. The sunray beamed through my sheer white curtains, bouncing off my mirror and almost blinding me. Oh no! I slept in my contacts. I looked in the mirror to check my eyes, and they were okay. What? My eyes weren't sealed shut, and I could see! From that moment on, I decided to sleep in my contacts so I would not have to deal with the stress of taking them out. As I was getting ready for the day, mom walked in and asked, "Did you put your contacts in?" "Yes ma'am," I replied. Saying "yes ma'am" and "no ma'am" was huge in my house. If you didn't say it, Mom was coming upside your head with force. "Good job, my baby, I'm proud of you. Let me call Shell and India to let them know how good you did." At that moment, I didn't feel sorry for lying. For starters, I did put them in my eyes. Who cares if it was yesterday? Lastly, Mom was proud of me! Therefore, I couldn't let her down. From that night on, I slept with my contacts in my eyes every night.

Chapter 3

The city pool was the hot spot during the summer. Everyone from all the surrounding neighborhoods would come to the pool and have a good time for $0.50. Between Ms. Mark's frozen cups and the city pool, I made sure I saved my quarters throughout the year in preparation for the summer. Earlier that year, at the local laundromat, run by my best friend Traci's uncle, I had found $4.00 worth of quarters. It was due to the old machines dropping quarters. I hope that wasn't stealing. The quarters were falling out of the washing machines. I saved the quarters and had them ready for the summer. Traci was throwing a pool party for her birthday. Her parties were always the best. They were very lavish events. Everyone who was anyone was there. Traci was short with a light complexion. She had long, beautiful black hair that went further than her bra strap. Traci reminded me of a Native American like Pocahontas. When she smiled, she had two dimples with pearly white teeth. She was turning 13 years old and had a figure like a 16-year-old junior in high school. All of the boys liked her, including the boys that were in high school. She was very popular, and she was my friend. I often wondered, "Why did the popular girls want to be my friend?" Traci knew the relaxed, goofy side of me. However, when other people would come around, I would go into my shell. She noticed that I would do this, so she would usually talk for me. I was comfortable with that. It was challenging for me to join conversations because of my awkwardness. I would have a perfect response in my head, but it would never come out the same way I thought it to myself. For example, one day at school, we were talking about how cute the guys were in David's crew.

Keshawn: "Girl, did y'all see them new J's David got over the Christmas break with that Carolina Jersey?"

Traci: "He know he fine with his stylish self, and he doesn't have a girlfriend, either."

My response: "I, I, I – would be his boyfriend."

Then, everybody would laugh. Also, there was the time our Spanish teacher was showing the class his country's flag, and I blurted out, "Your flag so plain." In most situations, I would shake my head, say "yeah" or smile. The day of the party, I was nervous and excited at the same time. She was bringing the small town out. She was going to have the best of the best at this pool party, with all the food ('cause her family is throwing down in the kitchen), a DJ ("Cause her cousin DJs at the local club), and all the cute boys. Hopefully, David will be there, because this will be my first time coming out without my glasses. Mom bought me a black floral swimsuit that crisscrossed in the back. The flowers on the swimsuit were pink and purple. I also had some short black gym shorts to put on with my swimsuit. Aunt Shell had just braided my hair to the back and added weave to the ends to make them longer. I was feeling cute for the party. I was going to the party with my first cousin, Tony. We were the same age. For that reason, he was closer to me than my little brothers. His dad, Big Tony, was my mother's younger brother, and he used to live with us. He ended up going to jail for a long time. I still don't know why, but mom gets sad every now and again when she thinks about him. He is her only brother. Tony's mother dropped us off at the party. The music from the party was pumping so loud that everyone in the parking lot heard it. The party was packed. Traci knew how to throw a party. The first person I spotted was Keshawn. She ran up to me, excited to see me, and pushed Tony on the forehead. He was her cousin as well. Keshawn had on this bad, bright pink two-piece swimsuit. Once again, she was another one looking like a 16-year-old, yet she was only 13. Why did I look so doggone young? Traci, in her colorful two-piece, came over to hug us. She was also looking hot and glowing; it was her birthday. All of the kids in middle school and even some high schoolers were there.

David and his crew were jumping off of the diving board, doing tricks. While gazing at David, Keshawn said, "Hey, let's go jump in!" Of course, I said no. I didn't know how to swim. Last summer, at the city pool, I was swimming underwater, and my old friend, Keke (yes, old because I don't play that), jumped on my back, and I almost drowned. I saw my life flash right before my eyes, but I saw someone wearing red shorts come to save me. Since then, I haven't swum underwater like that. I have huge trust issues. "Come on, JennyBoo!"

"Yeah, Jen! Stop being a punk. The lifeguards will catch you."

Why were Keshawn and Traci pressuring me? Were they trying to kill me? Keshawn rolled her eyes and said, "You know you want to go over there by David's fine self." Huh? How did she know I liked him? Traci joined in and egged me on. It worked. As I started walking over there, I locked eyes with David. I started waving with a big grin on my face, and then plop! I slipped and fell behind the diving board. I thought to myself, "Really, Jen? How could you fall before you even jump?" When I opened my eyes, everyone was surrounding me. I just closed my eyes again. I was dizzy, and the sky seemed blurry. I can't remember anything else after that, and honestly, I didn't want to remember anything. I remember my mom picking me up from the party. I sat in the car, crying my heart out. At that moment, Mom was compassionate. She didn't like to see any of her kids crying, and she didn't like knowing that our feelings were hurt. She rubbed my shoulder as she drove me to the ER. In our small town, there was only one hospital. I was pretty much a regular patient there due to my clumsiness. The wait wasn't that long. The doctor informed us that I had a little concussion as a result of my fall. Mom took care of me that night. I felt like her little girl again. Keshawn, Tony, and Traci called to check on me. I had told Mom that I didn't want to talk if anyone called. I think the embarrassment I felt outweighed the actual pain from the fall. I didn't want anyone to feel sorry for me or ask me, "Are you okay?" That night, my mom told me that Tony had almost drowned at the party after I had left. She said, "Yeah, Tony's butt was trying to show off in front of the knucklehead boys and almost killed himself." I felt terrible for him, as well, because I knew he wanted to be a part of David's crew. My embarrassment hurt me; I didn't have the energy to call Tony back to make sure he was okay.

Dear Diary,

I'm the stupidest, most awkward, clumsiest person EVER! I didn't even make it to the diving board without falling and busting my head. I know everyone wanted to laugh but didn't want to do it in front of my face. David will never look at me the same. I don't know if Traci and Keshawn will still want to be my friends. They're too popular to be friends with someone like me, anyway. I certainly don't need them to be my friends because they feel sorry for me. I'm going to stay to myself from now on. I don't deserve them as friends. Maybe, I'm thinking like this due to the concussion. I'm hurt. I should've followed my first thought and stayed where I was. I need to learn that I will never fit in. I'll always be the invisible girl. I'm starting to be okay with that.

Sincerely,

The Invisible Girl

The next day, they continued to call the house phone. I avoided them. I didn't want to talk to anyone about the incident. If I don't speak to them, I could act like it never happened. I don't think I reached out to Traci and Keshawn for the rest of the summer. I don't blame them for me falling, but I didn't want to hear what they had to say about it. Maybe, when I see them for our 8th-grade year, we can still be friends again. Perhaps we can all pretend like none of this ever happened.

Chapter 4

The July 4th holiday was big in my little town. It was a time when people got together for barbeques, fireworks, family laughs, and hanging out at Mason Park. These were fun times. In the small town I was from in Louisiana, segregation still existed. There was a white side of the city and a black part of town. I think everyone was free to go to any part of the town they chose. The two sides of town had just always been defined that way. That was just the way things were, and I don't think people questioned it, either. There was even a white park (Rushmore Park) and a black park (Mason Park). Rushmore Park had new playground equipment and an area that allowed you to meet up with friends for playdates. Our community would use that park for the birthday parties that we wanted to invite everyone from our class to, if you know what I mean. Living in a small town felt significant because it was so divided. There were parts of the city that we never ventured off to. The Mason Park had old, raggedy playground equipment. It didn't matter. We didn't go to the park to play, anyway. Sundays and holidays were times when everybody who was anybody would go to the park in their cute outfits and post up. "Post up" can mean anything, depending on where you live. Where I'm from, it meant being with your crew, "people watching." People would play their music loud from their old school cars. Some of the former basketball players would play basketball. To play on this court, you had to have been someone great in high school or at least be someone up and coming on the school's team. Most of the older men on the court were exceptional throughout their high school days, but none of them pursued their basketball dreams after that. That was common here. People who were famous (in our small town) for sports or school didn't make much of themselves after that. They would remind all the youngins how they were something in high school.

Even though we lived in Louisiana, we loved Texas music. It was a part of our culture in this small town in Louisiana. Artists like Z-Ro, Trae the Truth, DJ Screw, and Lil Keke, just to name a few, were what everyone jammed to. If you heard, "Slow, loud and bang, all in my truck," you knew there was a party somewhere. Not only did we like our music loud, but it also had to be chopped and screwed. Now, when it came to the music,

I loved it all. It was my way of fitting in. I could rap every word. When I listened to rap music, I would feel like a female boss that could potentially be a drug lord or someone big, making real money moves. Music would take me to another place, a dangerous but fun one. Tony and I bonded over music because he aspired to be a rapper. When India, Tony, and I would be together, we would freestyle, or help Tony make up raps. During the summer, I slept with the window open. In the window, there was a box fan so that I could let in a cool breeze on the hot summer days. Awakened by smoke creeping through my window. It wasn't just any smoke; it was smoke from the barbeque grill. Yes, it was the 4th of July. I was excited because we could finally pop the fireworks that Gary stinky booty self got us. I can't even lie, his barbeque was amazing. I enjoyed when he was on the grill because he was pleasant to be around for the holidays. As I looked out of my window, I saw Lil Gary and Torian shooting each other with water guns. I walked into the kitchen, where Mom was preparing breakfast. Yes, the smell of eggs, grits, pan sausages, and pancake "shole" smelled good to me. Mom said, "Jen, don't forget you have a track meet this weekend." "Yes ma'am," I replied. Mom always kept us busy, mainly because she did not want us getting into trouble in the neighborhood. It was too late for Lil Gary. Lil Gary did whatever he wanted to do and dealt with the consequences later. People would ask me if I was Lil Gary's big sister. I'm pretty sure that wasn't how it was supposed to go. Still, Lil Gary was well-known everywhere he went, no matter if it was for something good or bad. Most of the time, it was something terrible.

He was always stealing something from somebody. He would even take the parts off Torian's bicycle and mine to sell them. We still don't know what he would do with the money. At the same time, Lil Gary was giving, as well. Maybe he provided us with things because he felt sorry for stealing from us. Even though he was terrible, I still had his back. I remembered one time, this big kid my age was trying to fight him. Now Lil Gary was precisely that, little. So I couldn't let this big boy hurt my brother. I stepped up and ended up getting my lip busted. He still didn't mess with Lil Gary or me again. We all became friends after that.

After breakfast, I decided to get ready for the day. Mom and I were going to visit Baby Gracie at Aunt Shell's, and before that, we ate some of Gary's good ole barbeque. I got dressed fast, and I decided to go outside to wait for Mom to finish getting ready. I had on some short white shorts with a yellow and white plaid shirt. It tied in the front, and it showed a little stomach. I wore a cute pair of white sandals. I knew it was going to take at least another hour for Mom to get ready. She would always take forever, so I had time to waste. It didn't matter what the situation was; she needed two hours minimum to get ready. As I was sitting on the steps watching cars pass by, my cousin, Earl J, came over. He lived right across the street. He was Lil Gary's age, but Earl J loved to bother me. I was feeling too cute in my white outfit, so I didn't want to play with him today. I had places to go and people to see. I should've been in the house with my white clothes on, but I was too nosey. I knew people had families coming in from out of town. I just wanted to see everything and people watch. That was something we didn't get to do that often. As I minded my own business, Earl J came towards me with an RC can in his hand. "I'll waste this soda on you," he said. See, this was the kind of stuff that he would do. I wasn't in the mood to deal with him. I responded, "Do it if you're bad enough." Do you know what this snot-nosed, big-headed little boy did to me? He poured some on my feet to be funny. As I got up to chase him, he opened the gate door to run away from me. In the process, he slammed the gate, and it hit my toe. I was furious; once I had caught him, I slapped him on the head a few times. When I had finished with him, my toe was still in pain. There was a throbbing, piercing pain in my index toe. You know the one next to the big toe? I cried out for Mom, and she came out of her room, confused. She yelled, "What the hell is wrong with you?" I bellowed, "My toe!" As the tears rolled down my face, she gave me some ice to put on my toe and some aspirin to help ease the pain. Then, she told me to stay off of my foot until my toe felt better. I limped to my room and went to sleep. When I woke up, it was late in the evening, and everyone was outside. My toe was still in pain, but I sucked it up and went outside to pop fireworks. I didn't have much fun that day because of the pain. I didn't want to ruin anyone else's fun either, so I sucked it up. I didn't make it out to see Gracie, Mason Park, or any other family members. However, I was wasn't going to miss the barbeque. For a day that was supposed to be so much fun for me, it turned out to suck, which seemed to be the theme of my entire summer. The weekend of the track meet, my toe was still in pain. I told Mom I thought my toe was broke.

Once again, she didn't believe me. At that point, I thought it was pointless to tell her anything else. She was only going to think I was lying. I don't know how I ended up on the track team or even at this track meet. The coach was friends with my mom, and he assumed I could run fast because of my stature. Being a tall, slim, African American female with long legs makes people assume that you're this amazing athlete. I wasn't a horrible athlete, but I wasn't great either. I was pretty mediocre. If it were up to me, I would write poems and watch TV all day. The coach had me running the 100-meter dash in the race. This race was typically for speedy runners, and I knew in my heart, soul, and mind that I wasn't going to do well in this race. I tried explaining to Coach that I couldn't do this. I told him that my toe was hurting badly. He grinned and said,

"You're nervous. You can do this." During the entire track meet, I sat in the bleachers, nervously watching all of the other races. I was sweating profusely even before the race had begun. The race was in another small town, and no one from my family had shown up to support me. I was excited about that, at least. I couldn't deal with the embarrassment from them. I could at least pretend that I had done okay since they weren't here to witness the massacre that was about to happen to me on the track. Once it was my turn to race, I limped over to Lane 5. I was in the third heat of the 100-meter race for the middle school girls. There were only 6 of us in the heat. The countdown began: "5, 4, 3, 2, 1..." I don't remember anything after that except for limping into last place, crying because of the pain. Coach hugged me and told me that it was okay. I asked his assistant to check on my toe. It was swollen and red. I knew something was seriously wrong with my toe, but no one wanted to believe me. This summer was teaching me to be more truthful. After the race, we went out to eat at McDonald's. When mom came to pick me up from the initial meeting spot, the coach told her about my toe. She immediately brought me to my favorite place, the ER. I really became a regular at this place. It was like a home away from home that I didn't want to visit anymore this summer. The doctor told us that my toe was broken, and there isn't much that you can do about a broken toe. Mom replied, "I knew that! That's why I didn't want to bring you." I laughed to myself and smiled at her. The doctor wrapped my toes and prescribed me some pain pills. He told me to stay off of my foot as much as I could. Then, he sent me on my merry way. The car ride home was silent, and the rest of the evening was quiet between us. I knew Mom felt bad about not believing me or taking me sooner to the ER. It was all good. I'm not in as much pain anymore and I wasn't mad at my mom.

Dear Diary,

Can you believe I ran in a track meet with a broken toe? Well, I didn't do much running. I just limped across the finish line. When I think about it, all I could do is laugh, because it was a great excuse to explain why I lost. I was going to lose anyway. I'm not even fast. They can let the long legs fool them. These legs are slow. Lol. I know mom felt terrible, and for some reason, I feel sorry that she feels awful. I know that she wouldn't want anything wrong to happen to me. I walked around here with a broken toe for a week. Maybe I'm stronger than I think or addicted to aspirin. Anyway, today ended up being a good day.

Sincerely,

The Invisible Girl

Chapter 5

Another thing I enjoyed about the summertime was visiting my grandparents. Mainly, since my cousins, Priss and CJ, lived there. I would visit them on weekends during the school year. During the summertime, I could go there any day or at any time. My grandparents were pretty cool to say that they were old. Mawmee and Paw were my father's parents. Even though I didn't have a relationship with my father, Mawmee and Paw loved and accepted me as their grandchild. Often, I made excuses for my father for being absent from my life. I mainly gave him the benefit of the doubt since he didn't even know about me until I was three months old. I would often tell my grandfather he was my dad because we had a special bond. He treated my cousin, Priss, and I like his daughters. My grandparents had six sons. That's why Mawmee was one tough cookie. My grandmother was this beautiful, brown-skinned older woman. She was thick in all of the right places with a humongous booty. Mawmee's booty was enormous; it would hang off of the seat of the piano bench. She would have different-colored hair every time I saw her. I think it was because she was trying to hide her gray hairs. However, the colors would never turn out how she wanted. It could be green, purple, and blueish, to name a few. She would wear these beautiful suits for every occasion. She would order her skirt suits from some magazine that all the ladies in our church used. I never saw her wear the same thing twice. Mawmee and I would have the best conversations. I could tell her anything, and she would laugh or shake her head at me. One day she was talking to Priss and me about saving ourselves for marriage and how it's an honor to wait. I told her I didn't want to wait because I needed to know how it felt before I got married. I then asked her, "What if you wait, and you don't like it?" She chuckled, "I waited for Paw, and you see we've been married for 40 years." I enjoyed being honest and open with Mawmee because I wasn't able to have these conversations with my mother. Paw was one smooth man. He had a gray afro, with a bald shiny piece in the middle. He was just a cool, laid-back man who enjoyed cooking, chewing tobacco, and watching sports. I would often wonder how they could love me so much when my father barely acknowledged me. Even my uncles would spend time with me. I had a special relationship with all of them while I felt like I was never good enough for my father. I was his only child for the longest. Now, I have a little sister and a brand new, baby brother. Even though my father was absent, my mother still encouraged me to form a relationship with him. Now that I was 13 years old, I was starting to hate my father. I was tired of him always making empty promises and leaving me hanging. The last time he disappointed me was in April when he promised to get me another TV after lightning struck mine one night during the storm. He bought it for me that previous Christmas, and it didn't make it a year before it broke. He was so inconsistent that I never knew when he was going actually to keep his word. With every year, every promise, hatred grew in my heart. Even though I had those feelings, I would still give him a chance. I guess there was still a piece of me that wanted to be accepted by him. Although I had family that displayed and expressed how much they loved me, I still longed for it from my father. I couldn't even call him dad, father, daddy, or papa; I would say: "Hey." Nothing felt natural with him. I still wanted it to so bad. I was invisible to him. Everyone would tell me how much I resembled him. It was mainly because of my nose. We both had big noses. Paw had a huge nose, too. I think our noses were inherited. Everyone would say I got my clumsiness from him. That explained so much. Another thing we shared was the fact that we were regulars in the ER. We also shared the fact that we were both cross-eyed when talking to people. It was a struggle for me to talk to people and look at them eye to eye. People tell me that I would look up or away when I said things. I didn't even realize when I did it. I wished we were able to share those stories. I would have someone to relate to and not feel as awkward. I knew that my dad was just like me. It's hard being awkward. Other people can rarely connect to your quirkiness

Dear Diary,

    Being surrounded by people I love, I still feel unloved. I feel abandoned by my father because he moved on to his second wife and third child. What about me? Why am I always an afterthought? I try to be strong and forget he exists, but it's so hard. I want him to love me like I love him, but he pays me no attention. I'm brokenhearted because I haven't heard from him since April. I don't care about the damn TV; I want to be around him. I need him. He always leaves me feeling helpless.

Sincerely,

The Invisible Girl

Chapter 6

For most of July, I spent my days with my cousins, Priss and CJ, since they were home for the rest of the summer. Priss was one year older than me, and CJ was one year older than her. We all got along like we were the same age. Priss and CJ's mother lived in Maryland, and their father was my dad's brother. He couldn't take care of them because he was on drugs very badly. He was continuously in and out of jail, so our grandparents had raised them since they were babies. Priss was everyone's favorite. She was a pretty, caramel-skinned teenager with beautiful, long, wavy hair. Even though she was very soft-spoken, she had the strength of a man. She would beat CJ up all of the time, and he was the oldest. Whenever CJ would get into arguments with other boys in the neighborhood, Priss would always beat the boys up for messing with her brother. CJ was the jokester of the family. He was always running around pranking and cracking jokes on people. He was hilarious too. That's why the boys always wanted to fight him. He would crack so many jokes on them; they would get mad and want to fight him. My cousins were the best. We would have so much fun together. It felt good to hang out with people my age. The only thing was, we would have to sneak to watch BET and MTV or even listen to R&B and rap. My grandparents didn't allow secular music or ungodly things in their house. My grandmother would smoke a pack of Kools cigarettes all day and gossip about people with her church friends. That's a whole other story. I never said it out loud though because my mouth was too smart. We would have to wait until they were asleep to put the TV on to watch BET Uncut or even Cinemax. We had to figure out what the people were doing through the gray, wiggly lines and static. We would make sure the volume was meager. My grandfather would sleep very lightly and fall asleep in his recliner most nights. We would also sneak and call boys from the church on the phone. We weren't allowed to talk on the phone beyond 7 p.m., and we couldn't talk to boys at all. With all the rules, I don't know why I loved going over to my grandparents' house. My brother was born on July 20, and he was finally coming home from the hospital. We were going to visit him at my dad and his new wife's house. My dad was now married to his second wife. She was nice to me. She had two other kids besides my baby brother. When I would occasionally come around, she would make me feel comfortable. Her kids were cool, too. She had two sons. They were between the ages of Lil Gary and Torian. They didn't bother me like my brothers did. I guess it was because I wasn't around them as much. It was the first time I was going to my dad's house. My little head had so many thoughts and emotions running through it at one time. I wanted to be excited about going to his house, but I had the glare of jealousy clouding me. There was a piece of me that wished I could stay with him. I wanted to know how it would feel to have my father in the house with me. My dad rented a house from my grandmother. It was the house she grew up in and inherited from her family. It looked like she grew up in the house, too. It was an ancient house that was very, very old. It was so old that the wood was falling apart down at the bottom of the house. The house was painted a royal blue with a white trim. It was so old that the house had a front porch full of old appliances that needed to be thrown out. When you entered the front door, there was the living room and a door that led to the bedroom. After my grandparents, CJ, and Priss had walked in, I dragged my feet along the floor as I entered. It was a constant battle for me between how I felt on the inside versus how I displayed it on the outside. When I walked in, I was greeted by him. He came over to hug me. He said, "Baby girl, come meet you baby brother, Donnie." When I glanced at him, he was not cute at all. I never thought babies were cute when they were first born. Except for Gracie, she was beautiful, but Donnie still looked like an embryo in the womb. I thought that this couldn't have possibly been my brother. As I glanced at him, he smiled at me. It smiled as if he knew I was his big sister, that smile helped me open up to the situation. Baby Donnie was innocent, and I didn't have to think negatively about him even if it was true. "Do you want to hold him," this deep raspy voice uttered? I didn't even look up. I just responded yes. A piece of me was happy to have another brother. Hopefully, he wouldn't be as bad as Lil Gary and Torian. Even if he is, I'll still love him, because I still love them knuckleheads. We spent the entire day over there, and it was fun. I enjoyed my time spent at my father's house. Still, I knew the feeling wouldn't last for long. I knew I wouldn't see him again for a long time. I wished I could have spent more time with him. Even if I expressed this to him, he wasn't going to do anything but make broken promises and apologize for the last time he had lied to me. At the age of thirteen, I was tired of hearing the same old excuses. That evening, my grandparents dropped me off at home because they were going out of town for a week to visit Paw's sister. Unfortunately, they didn't have room for me to come this time. I was disappointed because I really didn't want to go home without my mom there. She was out with my nanny, and Gary was home with the boys. As I waved goodbye to my grandparents, Priss, and CJ, tears rolled down my face. It certainly was not because I would miss them; it was because I would have to be here with the monster. As I stood on the porch with the screen door open, I heard a low, deep voice say, "Close that doggone door." I rolled my eyes and mumbled, "Here we go with this mess." As soon as I walked through the living room, I fell straight on my face. As I looked up, I saw Torian's face turning red from laughing so hard. He even had tears streaming down his face. I got up really quickly and started punching Lil Gary in the head. I was punching him with everything I had because I was tired of him messing with me. I couldn't even barely get in the house before he started picking at me. He was yelling, "get your fat self off of me. You stink! Daddy!" Gary came out with the belt swinging. He hit me across my back really hard. I turned around and pushed him. Before you'd know it, I yelled, "Get your damn hands off me!" Then, I ran out of the house, walking down Bill Street as the sun began to set, and the street lights came on. I was so angry I walked to my daddy's house. I had never gone over there by myself, and he didn't live that far from me. His house was maybe seven blocks away from where I lived. Living in a small town, we had everything close to everything else. As I approached the door, my heart started pounding. However, as soon as I was about to knock, I decided to head back home. I didn't want him or his wife in my business. I wasn't ready to talk him about my personal feelings. It seemed like the walk home took forever, because it was completely dark by the time I made it home. Now I understand why mom would tell us to be home before the street lights came on. When I got close, I heard my mom and Nanny yelling at Gary. He deserved every bit of it too. He had no right putting his hands on me. I'm not his child and never wanted to be. As I walked through the gate, my mom grabbed me as she examined my body and asked if I was okay. Once she noticed I was fine, she popped me upside my head. Then she fussed at me for cursing at an adult and putting hands on my brothers. I just said "yes ma'am," as I headed to my room. My brothers were in their room by this time so I was able to make it to my room without any more altercations. I really hated him. "Aaaah," I screamed while tears rolled down my face. I looked for my diary. It's been a while since I wrote, but I needed to let this out.

Dear Diary,

I wish Gary would die! He put his nasty, filthy hands on me, and I want to hurt him so bad. It's either him or me. I bet if I killed myself, my mom wouldn't even care. She cares about him more than me. I don't want to have anything else to do with any of them. I want to leave. I'm going to ask Mawmee and Paw if I can live with them. I can share a room with Priss. My mom would love to have her boys and their daddy here being a big ole, stupid-looking, happy family. I don't belong here with them. Gary already treats me like I don't exist. He hates me as much as I hate him. My brothers wouldn't care if I was here are not, and my momma always takes their side, anyway. I can't wait for my cousins Priss and CJ to come back. That way I'll be able to leave this raggedy house. This house is raggedy, and it's full of roaches. It was like they have become family members. I'm embarrassed to invite people over because we are over here living like we're poor. I won't miss this place!

Sincerely,

The Invisible Girl

Chapter 7

It's been a few weeks since the incident with Big Gary, and things were back to normal. He still stayed locked up in the room mumbling to himself, having the entire room reek of Old Spice and funky feet. Meanwhile, the boys were their usual selves. There were only a few weeks left of summer break. It was too hot to be outside. I felt so bored and lonely; I decided to sneak and make a BlankFace page. All of my friends had one last school year. My overprotective mom said I couldn't make one until I was in high school. I thought to myself, "I'm almost there, so it should be cool." I had an email address, though, because we needed to make one in my English class for this group project. I was going to have Keshawn email me a picture of the pool party because I didn't have a cell phone yet. I'll never forget the worst moment of my life. It happened at that pool party. I was feeling good that night, and I was going to make that picture my profile picture. I felt like a grandma asking my friend to email me the picture. My mom didn't want me to have a cell phone until I got a job. Living in a small town, not many people in middle schools had cell phones. Nevertheless, all of my friends did. I wanted one too, but my mom wasn't playing that. My uncle Charles gave me his old laptop last summer. I never pulled that thing out. I kept it under my bed along with everything else I tried to hide from Lil' Gary and Torian. Once they got their dirty, nasty hands on anything, it would be broken or messed up in some way. As I powered up the laptop, my mom peeked her head through the door. She startled me as she asked, "What are you doing?" I stuttered and responded, "Pl. Pl. Playing a game." I was nervous, and I hadn't even done anything wrong yet. She asked, "Okay, Are you hungry?" "No ma'am," I replied, as I watched her close my door. I typed in the BlankFace URL, and I got excited. I would always scroll on Keshawn's and Traci's pages, so it wasn't foreign to me. After I created the page, I began searching for people I knew. Of course, I requested Traci, KeShawn, India, and Tony to be my friends. I knew they were going to clown me because I finally got on social media. I didn't care. Then I saw David's page. My heart started pounding out of my chest. I haven't seen him since the infamous pool party incident, and I made sure to avoid him as much as possible. It was like I knew the times he would pass by on his bike to go to Cousin Leroy's house. I was glad to be at my grandparents' house most of July. I wouldn't run into David over there. However, this was BlankFace. We could be friends on here because I didn't have to talk to him in real life. So many thoughts were roaming through my head as I paced back and forth in the room. I said to myself, "Forget this," and I hit the request button. When the button went from the color green to the color red, I immediately started panicking. I thought to myself, "What did I do? Why did I do that? Watch him show all of his friends, and they talk about how clumsy and skinny I am." Ding! "Oh, my gosh, who could that be?" I slowly eased back towards the laptop. I had a red notification, and it was from Keshawn. Immediately, I was so nervous. I sent her a message asking her what she had been doing. I was finally over the party, and I missed my friends.

Keshawn replied: "Girl, let me find out you got a phone. Are you okay?"

Me: "Yeah, I'm good. I have been out of town with my grandparents."

Keshawn: "You could've called somebody. Traci and I be worried about your crazy self. How is your head feeling?"

Me: "Lol. My head is good. Was everybody making fun of me?"

Ding! Ding! More alerts were coming. Then I froze – David just sent me a message!

David: "Waddup Jen. You acting funny?"

Wait! Was that an accident? He said Jen, but he never talked to me like that before.

Me: "What do you mean?"

David: "I saw you peeking out of the window when I was riding pass ya house. "Why didn't you speak?"

Me: "I wasn't looking at you, I thought I heard my Mom's car pulling up. Lol"

David: "Lol. Whatever. You look good in your picture."

Me: "Thanks."

David: "You should come outside and talk to me. I'm about to pass by."

Me: "K."

"Ahaaaaaa!" David wanted to talk to me. He didn't even mention the party. Through all of my excitement, I didn't even realize all of the other notifications I had. I just left Keshawn hanging. I knew she would understand though. David wanted to see me. I ran into the bathroom leaving the laptop open and not worrying about Lil Gary or Torian messing with it. As soon as I sat on the toilet, I saw red dots again. The red spots were back. "What the heck could this be?" I thought to myself, "why are they back?' I didn't have time to panic. I put on one of mom's panty liners and threw the wrapper to the side, threw a bun in my hair, and put on some lip gloss. Finally, I ran outside to meet David. I had on blue jean shorts with a white tank top and grey Converse shoes. As I sat on the steps waiting for Davis, I watched the cars pass by. My little brothers were playing across the street at our cousins' house. The longer I waited, the more I started to think that David was playing with me. How could I fall for that like a fool? I got up to open the screen door, I wanted to forget that this ever happened. That's when I heard, "where are you going with that big butt?" Wait, I know that voice! I heard that voice very often in Mrs. Smith's class. I was grinning ear to ear, but I had to put on my mean mug. I didn't want him to think I was happy to see him. "What took you so long?" Then I rolled my eyes as hard as I could. I thought my eyes were stuck to my eyelids. David said, "Whatever! So where do you think you are going?" I responded, "I'm going in the house because you took too long to get here." He replied, "You know you wanted to see me." We didn't even get to talk much before I got this sharp pain in my stomach. It was aching and tightening up. It was a feeling that I couldn't explain. I felt like I needed to go lay down. I told David I didn't feel good and he made a joke saying that I had to do number 2. I laughed as I went into the house. As I was going in the house, I heard him yell, "Hit me up on BlankFace!" I ran to my room to lay down. That's when I saw my mom with the panty liner papers in her hand, and she was looking at my laptop. I just froze in the doorway. At that moment, I knew that my life was over. My mom would always tell me, "I brought you into this world, and I'll take you out." At this moment, I believed her. All I could hear was her saying, "you think you're grown huh?" I couldn't respond. I just stood there as tears rolled down my eyes. I was so terrified about this butt whooping I was about to receive; I forgot my stomach was in pain. The pain my mom was going to deliver was far worse. "So, you can't talk now? Do you want me to make you talk?" I said," What do you mean?" Then she said, "Now you want to play dumb. Go get a switch." I pleaded with my mom. "No mom, please. My stomach is hurting, and I have red dots in my underwear again." My mom froze. She didn't say anything. She just looked at me. She had tears rolling down her face. "Mom, I'm sorry," I said. "I know you said it wasn't my period but I don't know what's wrong with me. I am wrong for going in your stuff. I promise I won't do it again. I'm sorry for making a blank face page. I was bored. I missed my friends." Tears were streaming down both of our faces, but she didn't move. She just uttered, "My baby is growing up. I'm sorry I didn't believe you." "Did I hear that right? Did my mom say she was sorry? Was she okay," I thought to myself?

"Jen, I want the best for you, and I don't want you to end up like me. I don't want you to be a teen mom or feel like you have to rush into things as I did. I want you to take a bath and use one of my panty liners. I am going to take you to the store to get your pads, and some medicine for your stomach. The reason why your stomach feels like that is because you're having menstrual cramps. I'm also going to show you how to wash the red dots out of your underwear. Oh, and don't let the tears fool you, we're going to talk more about this BlankFace page you're going to deactivate it." All I could do was laugh, because my mom and I just shared a moment and I know she don't play. That day, my mom took me to the store and taught me how to take care of myself during "that time of the month." She shared stories with me about the time she started her cycle.

Things went back to normal as always.

Dear Diary,

It's time to go back to school already. The summer came and went so fast. Initially, I thought it was the worst summer ever, but it ended up being okay. I survived, and now I'm ready to start 8th grade. I guess. Lol. I even might have a boyfriend this school year. One thing I learned this summer is to take the good with the bad and trouble don't always last as Mawmee taught me. Until next time.

Sincerely,

The Invisible Girl

$13.95
ISBN 978-0-692-13877-9